# White Collar, Black Pumps

Dr. Sheria D. Rowe

Cover design: Jahlisa Misenheimer

Author Photo: Kasaundra Felder Photography, LLC

Publishing: Brookshire Book Group

ISBN: 978-0692808573

ISBN: 10:0692808574

# DEDICATION

This book is dedicated to my parents and siblings. My parents, William and Natasha Rowe, have supported me in everything I've done since I was a little girl. You two are my motivation, the reason I push so hard. My brothers, Morio, Rico, and Rashawn, thank you for always having my back.

I love you

Your Little Princess

# CONTENTS

# ACKNOWLEDGMENTS

I am very appreciative of all the people who supported me throughout my journey. For each person who gave me encouraging words or even a helping hand, thank you.

# 1
## PREPPING FOR THE BOARD MEETING

*Never underestimate the power of dreams and the*

*influence of the human spirit. We are all the same*

*in this notion: The potential for greatness lives*

*within each of us.*

—*Wilma Rudolph*

I remember the moment I recognized that,

as a woman, I would have challenges and barriers.

I also remember the moment I knew I wanted to

break them. I knew at a young age that I was

different. However, I did not truly understand it at that time, now I do.

I was born into a middle-class American family. While my dad was a banker, my mom happened to own a bookstore. I happen to be the only girl and have three brothers who are older than me.

As a little girl, in school and at home I was often confined to particularly roles and prevented from doing things I truly wanted to because I was not a "boy". "You're not supposed to do this," "Don't you know you're a girl," they would say. All this cautions however made me determined and stubborn to do the "unspeakable."

The challenges I encountered as a little girl were prepping me for what I would face as an adult. Workplace discrimination, being the token woman, gender differences, and sacrifices were challenges I faced throughout my time in corporate America. Little did I know that those same challenges would follow me as an entrepreneur. I remember seeing businesswomen walking around with perfectly tailored business suits accented with black pumps. Now, as an adult, black pumps accentuate any business suit I wear. My name is Dr. London Royster. I survived corporate America. I survived my failed relationships. I am surviving as an entrepreneur. I . . . am . . . surviving.

## 2
# FROM THE BOARDROOM TO BEING THE BOSS – DR. LONDON'S STORY

*You may encounter many defeats, but you must*

*not be defeated.*

*—Maya Angelou*

Immediately after earning a bachelor's degree in business administration, I started working as an entry-level business analyst for one of the most prestigious pharmaceutical companies in the city. I was a twenty-one-year-old woman, fresh out of college, with a corner cubicle in a top pharmaceutical company. For my first job, that was all I needed. I walked in the company ready to hit the ground running. My first week in the office was very informative. I was taking what I learned from college and placing those skills directly into my job, which made me have a sense of accomplishment.

After about a month at the company, I started to notice the lack of diversity in the office. As a college student, my business professors would tell me that as I am being interviewed for a job, be sure to interview them as well. During my initial interview, I should have asked the company about their diversity and culture within the organization.

I was the youngest and only African-American woman in the department. My direct manager was also a woman, but of European-American descent and slightly older than I was. To put this into perspective, that was the moment I knew there would be barriers ahead. During meetings, I always felt as if everyone was staring at my youthful face and bronzed brown skin, wondering why I was sitting in the boardroom. I always felt as if I did not belong, so I did not speak up much, even when asked for my input.

After being at the company for a while, my direct manager eventually became my first mentor. She spent countless hours with me and taught me the ins and outs of the corporate world and how to adapt. Little did I know that she was shaping me into leadership.

I remember, it was a Monday morning around 8:30a.m when the CEO of the company called my mentor into his office. About twenty minutes later, my mentor walked out. By the look on her face and her actions, I knew exactly what had happened. She gathered some of her belongings then proceeded to walk out of the office. Before she walked out of the back door, she turned around and walked over to me and said, "Be careful." I knew exactly what she meant. That was the last time I saw her.

Three days later, my new direct manager was a male with little experience in the industry, and I was not even surprised. Now, let us fast forward a little. A few months after my mentor was let go, she was able to get in touch with me through social media. She explained to me she was let go due to budget cuts. Interesting, right?

Roughly a year after the firing of my mentor, my time at the company was coming to an end as well. This was a time when the economy was not doing so well and companies were suffering, especially start-ups. My time with the company I once walked in with high hopes came to an end. I was called into the human resource office and was told the company had to make budget cuts, and I was one of the several employees included. I loved my job and hated that I was being let go, but I knew the actual reason.

A few months after I was laid off at the pharmaceutical company, I obtained a position as a senior business analyst at a mid-sized media relations company. My direct manager during this time was an older black woman who had been in the exact same position for twenty-one years. This company was the only organization she had ever worked for. During a one-on-one lunch meeting with her, I asked why she never wanted to move up in the company. She simply smiled and said, "I did move up once." She then began to tell me how she had been in senior management but after she decided to start a family, she was asked to step down. Out of about one hundred employees at the company, only two women were in management. I knew I was not going to be at that company long due to the difficulty of advancement. After only nine months at the company, I resigned.

# 3
# A NEW CHAPTER

*Challenges make you discover things about*

*yourself that you really never knew.*

—*Cicely Tyson*

I earned my master's degree and was now a senior business analyst at a start-up company, which enabled me to wear several different hats. In addition to my senior business analyst duties, I assisted the data integration implementation team, new hire training, and other key positions. I always remembered what my first mentor taught me about leadership: as women, we typically have to work twice as hard as our male counterparts, even if that means having several different roles in an organization.

I always had a personal goal to earn my doctorate degree. After a year at the company, I decided to enroll in a PhD program. I was able to manage a full-time job and being a full-time student. It was a very stressful time for me, and during the time I was working toward my degree, I developed chronic migraines. I would work countless hours at my full-time job and use lunch breaks to conduct research and write my dissertation. I also decided to teach a business course during the evening, in addition to my full load of responsibilities. On a good day, I would get home from work and teaching around 10:00

p.m. I would then have dinner for about thirty minutes and then begin researching and writing. My social life went down the drain and I barely had any me time but for me it was worth the struggle. To get to the top, sacrifices have to be made. This hectic schedule went on for about a year, then I decided that teaching in the evenings was too much. I cleared my teaching responsibility from my plate hoping to have time for other things.

After being at the company for three years, I realized I was in the same senior business analyst position that I was in when I started. After receiving excellent annual reviews for the past three years, I decided to express my concerns with my direct manager. My manager was a white male with very little education. He could barely articulate his words and seemed to rarely be available. He explained to me I was up for a promotion, so I immediately began training. After six months of extensive training, I was then told that the company did not have the budget to promote me into a director position. I was thinking, "I've heard this before . . . another budget issue." Three additional months went by, and the company began to hire additional analysts. Two months after the mass hiring, one of the new analysts became a director.

I remember working late in the office one Friday night, assuming I was alone. I needed a client file from our secured file room, which was located toward the back of the building. I unlocked the door, walked in, and saw my manager and the newly promoted director proving to me how she was promoted so quickly. Thank God they didn't hear me, so I was able to quietly walk back out without being noticed. I went back to my office and left for the remainder of the evening.

The entire drive home, I was furious. I had put in so much effort into the company and yet others had been put over me. At that moment, during my drive, I knew I wanted to break the barriers that were holding me back from career advancement. That was when I decided to take a risk, to become an entrepreneur.

My first step was to resign and it was a huge risk even with my degrees, as the job market was shaky. I remember many telling me not to quit, that it was something I was going to regret in time to come, but I was determined. I had had enough of being stepped on by many not because they did not know my worth but because I was a woman.

I resigned from the company and started my own small advertising agency. I wanted to take my education, skills, and experience to create my own opportunity. By far, it was one of the best decisions I have made.

# 4
# THE TOKEN WOMAN – SHELLEY'S STORY

*I don't go by the rule book. I lead from the heart,*

*not the head.*

*—Princess Diana*

Shelley is an old friend I met during my freshman year in high school. She has always been outgoing, and out of all my friends, the most popular. In high school, she was the captain of the varsity cheerleading team, member of the debate team, and maintained a 4.0 GPA. As adults, we have always made time for our friendship, even with our busy schedule, careers, and family responsibilities. She has always been the type of woman who is about her business and the type of woman you would want in your inner circle. Since high school, we would always share our most private secrets, and we knew each other's most hidden skeletons. After we graduated from high school, we ended up attending different colleges. Shelley went to North Carolina Central University, and I went to Spelman College in Georgia. My original choice was NC Central, but Spelman offered me a full scholarship for the entire four years of my matriculation.

After we both graduated from college, our jobs brought us back together in the same city; the Queen City… we've been inseparable since.

While at NC Central, Shelley met the man that she ended up marrying. Her husband, Dr. Eli McGrady, is an emergency room physician, and they have a son, Mason, who is six. Eli stands six foot two and has a nicely shaved baldhead, with a beard and thick eyebrows. He rarely wore his wedding ring, which I just assumed was because of sanitation reasons and the nature of his job in the emergency room. He is also the type of man that puts more energy into his career than his own family. I have observed the behavior myself as well as Shelley discussing it during our girl-talk sessions.

The first time I met Eli, I was a freshman in college. Shelley introduced him to her inner circle during a Labor Day cookout in our hometown. From day one, I never really trusted him. It also did not help that I knew about some of the skeletons in his closet. One particular incident I remember is that I was on a dating site and saw his profile pop up. It was a little confusing to me that he was married but on a dating site. I never shared with Shelly what I saw, but it was my confirmation not to trust him. However, even with his faults and dishonesty, the only thing I like about him is that he has been able to stand by my friend's side.

Shelley attended law school at the University of North Carolina-Chapel Hill immediately after graduating from NC Central. Using her many corporate connections, Shelley was hired immediately after law school at Miller and Associates Law Firm. She finished law school at the top of her class, so it was destined for her to become a successful attorney at one of the most prestigious law firms in Charlotte.

Shelley and Eli had a system that apparently worked for them and their schedules. Shelley worked during the day, and Eli worked nights at the hospital. On many occasions, he would be on call, which sometimes caused a rift in their relationship. Every day before leaving home for work, Shelley would kiss Eli, tell him how much she loved him, then hug Mason before walking out the door. It was always evident how much she loved her family, by the affection she displayed. Their hectic schedules forced them to make the decision to hire a full-time, live-in nanny. In the beginning, Shelley was not the biggest fan of having a live-in nanny, because of her personal reservations but it was important for them to continue their career and have a stable family. They both interviewed several options and ended up choosing Ms. Lucille. She was a retiree from the public school system with three children and five grandchildren. She was perfect for the job.

During the day, Shelley would be in the office and Eli spent the majority of his time home resting. They both had very high-demand careers, which made it difficult for them to spend the time they yearned for together. By the time Shelley came home from work, Eli was on his way out. This hectic schedule had been going on for quite some time, and for Shelly, trying to balance her career and family responsibilities was beginning to be too much. She was tired.

# 5
## GLASS BREAKS, BUT I DON'T

*Those who complain about glass ceiling should*

*keep in mind that glass can be shattered if one*

*strikes hard enough and long enough.*

—*Author Unknown*

I never understood why my elders would not support receiving professional help from a licensed therapist. Was it because they were always taught to keep a private life and deal with their issues behind closed doors? I will never know.

Over a much-needed cocktail and girl-talk session with Shelley, she disclosed to me the therapy sessions she and Eli were attending. Of course, I gave her "the look" while asking why they were attending sessions.

Shelley responded saying, "Sometimes you have to receive professional advice on how to deal with life's changes and situations." Still confused about what life changes and situations she was referring to, I just left it alone. She explained to me how productive the sessions were and that I should try therapy. I have never been opposed to therapy. I just never took the step to go.

We went on to talk about my work which was doing really good for itself.

"How's Marcel doing?" Shelley asked.

She was referring to my attorney. Marcel is a handsome man, around six foot with a good-looking body. It is not something anyone can miss. He is really good at his work and came in highly recommended by Shelley, who was my original company lawyer. Her workload was however too much and as a good friend I had to take some stress off of her.

"He's good," I told her with a shrug.

"You should go out with him," she said with a smile.

I shook my head. He was a good man no doubt but the last thing I needed at the moment was a relationship. I was going through so much and was not completely over the last man I had been heavily involved with.

Before we separated, I made sure to take the details of the therapist of Shelley's whom I decided to pay a visit to and try.

Dr. Alexandria's office was located in the heart of uptown Charlotte. The location was perfect. My advertising agency was just a few blocks down the road, so it was easy access to and from sessions, and I could even walk. Anxiously waiting for my session to begin, I could not stop tapping my foot on the perfectly polished hardwood floors in the waiting room. All I could think of was how it was going to go and what would be the outcome. I think I was even excited since it was my first time of seeing a therapist.

A few minutes later, a short and very thin woman with long, nicely layered dirty-blonde hair called my name and asked me to follow her. Dr. Alexandria directed me to a seat and pulled out a thick notebook. She then said, "London, what brought you in today?" I explained that I was referred by one of her patients and wanted to see what I could get out of the sessions.

The session started with me introducing myself to her and providing a quick snapshot of my life. I told her of my dad who had retired and my mom who was still managing the bookstore. Two of my brothers were married with kids and one was divorced. I was single and had not been on a date in a long while thanks to my company, which I was trying to get off the ground. Thirty minutes went by, and I had told her about my family, career, and relationships. Coming to a close, Dr. Alexandria said, "Tell me more about Josiah."

I replied, "He's my ex-boyfriend." At that moment, I wondered why I had even told her about him in the first place when talking about my past relationships. I glanced over at the clock, and the hour session was coming to an end. "Dr. Alexandria, I'm sorry, but I have to go. I will schedule our next session with your secretary," I said getting up very eager to leave.

Dr. Alexandria said, "We need to continue this conversation in our next session."

I had already slammed the office door before she could even finish her sentence.

# 6
## THIS IS A MAN'S WORLD – OR NOT

*A woman with a voice, is by definition, a strong
woman.*

—*Melinda Gates*

Shelley stormed in the courtroom a little after
9:45a.m. Her client's case was called thirty
minutes prior. After finding out another attorney
had assisted her client, Shelley walked back to her
office. As soon as she walked in the door,
Andrew Miller, managing partner of the firm,
called her into his office. Andrew began the
conversation stating how disappointed he was in

Shelley for missing an important court date, and, more importantly, how they just lost a client due to her tardiness.

"Andrew," said Shelley, "I sincerely apologize. I was running behind from a doctor's appointment this morning. Is there any way I can make this right?" Andrew proceeded to tell her the importance of time management and reminded Shelley that she was up for partner at the firm. Any mistakes could affect the partnership.

For the remainder of the day, Shelley was completely disappointed in herself for losing a client. Making partner was a goal of hers since she had stepped foot in the firm. Shelley never realized how real the "token" concept was, until she became one. Being the only female attorney in the firm, she was being held to higher standards than those of her male counterparts. After leaving the office that evening, Shelley asked herself why.

On many occasions, I have been in her office during lunch or just to stop by to say hi, but Andrew was never there. He was typically busy taking lavish trips with his wife or attending sporting games with other colleagues while Shelley was in the office taking care of his cases and hers. She had always been a hard worker and just a mistake, she was penalized for it.

This was one of the very few days her husband was off work, so Shelley left the office at a reasonable time in order to spend time with him and Mason. Shelley walked into the house and noticed the aroma of Italian food. Continuing to walk into the kitchen, she saw Eli standing over the stove with nothing on but the custom apron she gave him the previous year as a Christmas gift. Eli loved to cook. If he had not gone into the medical field, his next option would have been to become a chef. Shelley stood in the middle of the kitchen shocked, thinking, "He has cooked!" Eli poured Shelley a glass of her favorite wine, Pinot Grigio, and told her to have a seat. Shelley asked where Mason was.

"He's with my parents until tomorrow morning," said Eli.

During dinner, Shelley told Eli about her missed court case and how she had placed her position as a partner in jeopardy. "Eli, I don't understand how I was late to one case my entire career and disciplined for it. Other attorneys have been late or not even shown up, and haven't been treated the way I was. I guarantee if I was a man, I would not have been questioned."

Eli nodded and patted her on the back. This was not the first time Shelley would complain about being discriminated at work due to her sex. Several times she had been given certain cases and not given some cases due to her being a female. A few times, she had brought this up to her boss but had only been ignored to the point that she had stopped "bothering" them.

Eli and Shelley finished dinner, cleaned up, and then decided to call it a night.

The next morning, Shelley called me to ask if I wanted to meet for brunch. We ended up meeting at a Mexican spot in midtown. Shelley had been looking forward to the weekend. Between the stress at work and not feeling well, all she wanted to do was rest and spend time with her family and friends.

The weather was perfect—the fall leaves starting to fall with the nice crisp air but still sunny skies with beaming rays. Shelley and I loved the fall season. We could bring out our best fashion, from booties shoes to blazers. I looked at Shelley and said, "Shelley, you look tired. Is everything okay?"

Shelley replied, "Yes, I'm just a little drained from work."

I could tell something was bothering her, but like always, I knew she would tell me in her own time. After a few moments of quietness, she said, "I wonder how difficult it would be to invest and open my own practice."

I was thinking in my head how random this was; Shelley loved her law firm. She had spent years assisting with building the firm, and now she was thinking of having her own?

I replied, "You know how I feel about entrepreneurship. Go for it! I did even though there were a lot of uncertainties but with where I am today, I have no regrets and know I won't." Shelley looked over at me and gave me a nod.

After finishing brunch, we said our usual goodbyes and went our separate ways.

# 7
# A NEGATIVE RETURN ON INVESTMENT

*Learning to love yourself, it is the greatest love of*

*all.*

—*Whitney Houston*

During the time I was approaching my last year of graduate school, I was also laid off at the pharmaceutical company. To me, the layoff was a blessing in disguise; I was able to focus on my school work and prepare for graduation. I was also forced to let go of other distractions in my life: Josiah.

Josiah is my ex-boyfriend and someone I thought I was going to spend the rest of my life with. He was exactly my type: six foot three, athletically built, desirable, and had a tattoo on his chest that made looking at him shirtless even better. He also had a smile that could make any woman want to smile back. We met during our freshman year in college. I had been at a bar waiting for some friends when he had joined me and asked to keep me company. He was charming and I gave him my number before I left that night.

It also helped that he was accomplished in his career as a senior engineer at one of top tech companies in the nation. I was aspiring for greater heights and so was he. He was the type of person one needs to push you up that level of success. I loved that man, and anyone who had ever been around us knew that as well. He was good to me in every way I can think of. He was romantic, caring and loving. There were times I would come back home stressed out and he knew what exactly to do to make me feel much better. It is sad to say that these days, it is hard to come across a man like Josiah.

Little did I know that what I thought was a close to perfect relationship, would end after three years, and I had no idea why. I literally stopped hearing from him, with no explanation and with no closure. I tried to reach out to him several times over the period of a month. I went over to his home a couple of times but he refused to see me. My calls and messages remained unanswered. After I did not receive a response back, I finally gave up. It was hard for me as I thought he was the love of my life, I had imagined us getting married and starting a new life but I had been wrong. I was deeply hurt and I remember crying over it for a while, I just could not believe that what I truly cherished was over and I had no reason what the reason was.

At one point, I was considering just leaving and moving away where I could start over. I wanted the hurt to go away. I was in a hopeless place that no one could take me from. Shelley came around and tried to talk me out of my depression but I was not ready. I remember a few days after, I looked into the mirror and did not like what I saw. My eyes were empty of any activity, of joy. I was not the person I had once been and it killed me. I decided then that it was Josiah's loss. I was going to move on with my life and the break up was just another hurdle in my journey in life.

From that point, I decided to focus solely on my career. There was a time in the relationship when I focused on "us" instead of "me." Sometimes, you can lose focus of your own goals and aspirations by helping others reach theirs. That's where I was in my life at that particular moment. I always thought that if I took care of Josiah, was attentive to his needs, and did all the things my mother told me on how to keep a man, that he would want to marry me one day. We talked about it, but he just was not ready.

When Dr. Alexandria asked about Josiah in our session, it sparked several different emotions: anger, disappointment, and betrayal, which I had buried deep down in my heart.

We had been broken up for about a year when I heard the news that I knew one day I would hear. It was a Friday evening, and I had just got settled in after dinner with a business partner. That was when I received a phone call from one of my college friends. I could tell by her tone that she was calling to tell me disturbing news. The conversation started with her asking me how I was doing and having general small talk. She then said, "I wanted to tell you before you saw it on social media or heard from someone who is not your friend. Josiah got married today."

I replied, "Thank you for telling me." We talked for another brief moment before ending the call.

I was not even surprised to hear about Josiah getting married. Yes, I was hurt, but I knew that life would go on. I was happy with how I reacted, there were no tears shed this time around. Besides, I was focused more than ever on my career goals. My company's growth was going remarkably, and I was surrounded by family and friends who supported me. I could not ask for more.

The next evening, I finally had the opportunity to soak everything in. I knew that I probably would not receive closure from Josiah, but I wanted to address him one last time. As part of my therapy sessions with Dr. Alexandria, I had been keeping a journal. I decided to write an e-mail, and that would be my closure once and for all for the Josiah chapter of my life. Before I typed the e-mail, I wrote what I wanted to say in my journal:

*Josiah, I first want to congratulate you on your recent nuptials. Marriage is a vow before God and your spouse. I pray that your union brings you the love and happiness that you deserve. I never understood your reasoning behind leaving and with no explanation. For a long time, I blamed myself, trying to figure out what exactly I did so wrong for*

*you to make the decision you made. Whatever the*

*reason, I forgive you. I no longer can beat myself*

*up trying to understand. I loved you, but I love*

*myself more, and because of the love I have, I had*

*to forgive myself. Again, I pray you receive the*

*same     love     that     God     has     for     you.*

—LR


It was time for me to schedule my next

appointment with Dr. Alexandria. I knew I had to

prepare for her to ask me about Josiah again and

that I would finally be ready to discuss.

# 8
# THE B WORD: BALANCE

*Life is a balance of holding on, letting go, and*

*knowing when to do which of the two.*

*—Author Unknown*

I did not realize how close it was to three o'clock. I had to rush out of my office and drive the three blocks that I would typically walk to my session with Dr. Alexandria. I finally decided to hire an assistant to help me organize client information, manage databases, and handle my scheduling. With me showing her the systems and databases, I had completely lost track of time.

I finally made it to my session fifteen minutes late. I walked into Dr. Alexandria's office suite and got comfortable, and tears started rolling down my eyes. Before Dr. Alexandria could even get a sentence out, I said, "You ever feel like the weight of the world is on your shoulders and there is nothing you can do about it?" That's how I felt. For the past three months, I had been feeling completely overwhelmed with a lot of things going on in my life. I was always taught to pray, during good and bad times. I prayed every morning and afternoon, before I went to bed, and several other times throughout the day, but I still felt heavy on the inside.

Dr. Alexandria asked me why I was feeling the way I was. I told her about my company's growth and how it was a little overwhelming, how I was worried about one of my brothers who was currently overseas due to the military, my parents in general, Josiah, and a multitude of other issues I was currently dealing with.

"How do you feel about Josiah getting married?" asked Dr. Alexandria. I told her exactly how I felt. I felt like a failure. It didn't affect me as much when I received the news, but now it had really soaked in. I invested so much time and energy into the relationship, but to him, it wasn't enough. I felt like him leaving me was a punishment. What I failed to tell Dr. Alexandria in our previous session was my difficulty in carrying a child. Josiah always talked about wanting several children. During our relationship,

I wasn't trying to get pregnant, but it happened. Eight weeks into the pregnancy, I miscarried. About a year later, I found out I was pregnant again. I again miscarried the baby. I was embarrassed. I was in love with a man who desperately desired children, but I was unable to carry them. So, yes, when I heard of his nuptials, I had many questions. Did he leave me and marry someone else because of my fertility issues, or was I just not good enough for him?

The session was coming to a close. Dr. Alexandria gave me two different assignments. The first was to pick up a book titled *God's Promises*, and the second was to compile a list. *God's Promises* is a book that directs you to different scriptures in the Bible for what you are dealing with. The list I had to compile had to consist of my priorities in the order of importance. At the end of the session, I gave Dr. Alexandria a hug and thanked her. I knew I had made the right decision by attending the therapy sessions.

After the session, I didn't even bother to go back into the office. Instead, I went home, mentally exhausted. After I settled in, I cooked dinner, showered, and began to prepare for the next day. Before calling it a night, I decided to start writing my list. The first priority on my list was God; I desired a closer relationship with him. As a child, I was forced to attend church, Bible study, Sunday school, church picnics, Halleluiah night, and anything else you can think of dealing with the church. Now as an adult, my relationship with God comes before anything else. I've dealt with too much not to give God my time. The second item on my list was family. My parents and siblings have always been supportive of me, and whatever they needed, I made them my priority. Over the years, I learned that the world can turn its back on you, but family will always be there. I grew up in a family-oriented household. My parents taught my siblings and me to always protect and be there for each other. To this day, we do just that. My third item was my career, my company. I shed blood, sweat, and tears for my company, and making it a priority was not an option. I had to sacrifice a lot for a vision that no one saw but myself. I finished compiling my list and realized something was wrong. I did not include myself.

The next day, I called Shelley and asked if we were still meeting for our standing happy-hour girl-talk time. We met at Chima Brazilian Steakhouse, our favorite. Shelley asked how my sessions were going with Dr. Alexandria. I told her that surprisingly, they were going really well. While waiting for our food and drinks to come out, I had to talk with Shelley about my upcoming birthday plans. "So, Shelley, my birthday is coming up in a few weeks."

"What plans do you have?" she asked.

Truth was that I did not really have a plan. I loved to celebrate my birthdays every year as they were a reminder of how far I have gone in life. Normally, a day at the spa or dinner at a restaurant would do, but this year was different. I have had a hard time as well as nice moments this year. I was going through a lot and needed some time away. It occurred to me that moment that I needed to travel, go somewhere far away where I could rediscover myself. Jamaica was the country that instantly came to my mind. And what good would it be traveling alone? Shelley had gone through a tough year too and needed a break. The vacation began to form in my mind.

"How about you come with me to Jamaica?" I asked.

I was disappointed when she quickly declined, telling me she was up for partner and could not afford to take time off, how Eli didn't have time off, that she didn't have anyone to take care of Mason, and any other excuse she could think of. I told Shelley that she hadn't been on vacation since she started working for the firm, and it was time for a break. We needed some alone time far away, it was something we both deserved. I asked her to think about it for a few days and get back with me for a definite answer; Shelley agreed. We finished with our food and drinks and went our separate ways.

Shelley got home only to find a note from Eli telling her he had to go into work a little earlier than usual. She released the nanny and put Mason to bed. She started to really think about the Jamaica trip that I had presented her with. The next morning, Shelley discussed the trip to

Jamaica with Eli. Surprisingly, he supported her going. She called me around 7:30a.m. as I was walking into my office. I could tell by the excitement in her voice that it was something I wanted to hear. Shelley told me that she talked to Eli and that we were going to Jamaica!

# 9
## ANNUAL LEAVE

*Fall in love with taking care of yourself; mind,*

*body, and spirit.*

*—Author Unknown*

Being in Jamaica was everything Shelley and I
needed. We both hadn't been able to take time
away from work due to our responsibilities and
obligations as adults. For the duration of our
vacation, we both agreed to not check our
business e-mails. We spent the majority of our
first day lounging on the beach and enjoying the
peace. I was extremely impressed with the clean,

clear blue water, hot sand between my toes, and the sun rays that reminded me of God's warm love he has for me. The view was nothing but amazing. It also helped that I was in beautiful Jamaica with my best friend, someone I have trusted and loved like a sister since my teenage years.

I knew something was bothering Shelley, but I've always had the "she'll talk to me when she's ready" approach to our friendship. When Shelley gets quiet and has a glazed look, I know she has a lot on her mind. Just as I thought, Shelley decided to open up when she was ready. We were sitting on the beach for dinner, and she turned to me and said, "London, you always told me that if I wasn't happy with a situation, to either walk away or find a way to fix it. I am now at my breaking point with my law firm."

Shelley continued to tell me that the passion she once had for Miller & Associates was leaving. "I love my career and the power I feel after winning a case, but I cannot continue to work for a company that is not willing to work for me. I am giving them my all and I have been doing so for a long time, but nothing I do is appreciated. It is as if I am being taken for granted and limited. This is a job that is supposed to treat me right, to make me feel excited every day I walk into the office. But I don't feel the way that I used to in my early days, it is like a burden, one I want off my head. "

I looked at her and gave her a nod, then told her, "At this point in your life and career, you need to do what you feel is best for you and your family."

Shelley looked at me, snickered, and said, "Hmm, family." She continued, "How do you tell the child you have been raising since birth that you're not really his mother? When the new baby arrives, Mason is getting old enough to realize he won't look like his 'baby sibling.'"

I gave Shelley a deep stare and asked, "New baby? Shelley, you're pregnant?"

Shelley replied with a nod and followed with a verbal reply of yes. "London, I was going to tell you before we came on vacation, but I knew we were going to have plenty of time to talk. Eli wants another child, I do too but I know that it is going to be stressful for the both of us. We will have to compromise and come to a mutual agreement about our careers because this baby will surely affect them."

Shelley continued and told me of how her doctor's appointments had been conflicting with work. Because Shelley was up for partner at her firm, any little mistake she made was noticed. "London, I don't want to have to choose between having a child and my career. One part of me is excited about the pregnancy, but the other side knows it will jeopardize my opportunity to make partner. Eli wouldn't understand the sacrifice I will be making."

I then asked her, "Shelley, does Eli know that you're pregnant?"

Shelley replied saying, "No."

I could clearly see that she was in a state of conflict. A child was coming and her job was on the line; it was a field which she truly loved and she had been wanting to make partner for a long time. I took her hand in mine and hugged her. We go through so much internal conflict that many don't know about. It is hard making choices but they have to be made. "We will make it through," I told her as well as myself.

For the remainder of the trip, Shelley and I continued to talk about the issues we were both dealing with in our lives. Having the conversations with Shelley made me realize that I wasn't the only woman that dealt with issues in the workplace. As I was lying in bed during our last night in Jamaica, I began to write in my journal:

> *Why do we, as women, have to sacrifice so much for our careers? Why does it seem we have to make a choice between family and our careers? We give up so much in order to please many and at the end of the day, we are left drained. You dream of who you want to be every since you were a kid, and work towards it but then at the end of the day you have to give it up. It is like we women don't have ambitions, as if we don't have something we want to achieve, we're just expected to let go of our dreams when the time comes. I no longer have much to say as I am lost for words. I*

*am fed up with the injustice that is going on. My*

*best friend is suffering, and I am not sure if I am*

*strong enough to help get her through.*


I remember one of my colleagues from corporate became pregnant during the most crucial time of her career. She was at the beginning stages of her divorce process when she found out that she was pregnant. She never told her soon-to-be ex-husband about the pregnancy; she quietly made the decision to end the pregnancy. The estranged couple finalized their divorce about eight months later. To this day, I wonder if their relationship would have been different if she had told her ex-husband about the pregnancy. My heart was heavy just thinking about Shelley and some of the major decisions she was going to have to make. Even though I knew she would make the best decision for herself and her family, I knew how it could take an emotional toll on her body.

I tried to make the rest of the trip eventful for the both of us. We had fun and felt free from all the stress back home. But the truth was that we knew we were going to return to those hurdles but now we had a positive mindset that everything was going to be fine.

Preparing to leave the beautiful Jamaican resort, I thought of how great of a trip this was. It was a form of therapy that we both needed.

# 10

# AN EMOTIONAL ROLLERCOASTER

*Healing begins where the wound was made.*

*—Alice Walker*

I was glad to be home, but knew I was in for a lot of long hours in the office. While I was away on vacation, my company gained two new corporate clients. Having a company that is experiencing rapid growth can be both challenging and exciting at the same time. The week after I returned from Jamaica, I scheduled a meeting with my attorney, Marcel and my mentor to discuss some company changes.

The three of us met at The Capital Grille in downtown Charlotte. I ordered my favorite, the all-natural herb roasted chicken, while Marcel and Santina ordered the sea bass. While we were eating dinner, the conversation was focused on the current state of my company. We talked about the rapid growth, hiring additional consultants, and the main reason I scheduled the dinner meeting: company expansion.

For a while, I had been thinking of expanding my advertising company to another city. After months of market research and ensuring the expansion would be conducive, I decided to open a second office in Los Angeles. Having offices in Charlotte and LA would help my company have continued growth. Marcel and

Santina agreed with the decision, and having their support was exactly what I was looking for. In the process of conducting market research, I found an office space in the heart of downtown LA. It was located on the fourth floor and overlooked the city. Marcel agreed to travel with me to LA so we could finalize all the legal documentation for the space and start moving furniture in.

While I was busy prepping for my Los Angeles travel, Shelley was also busy in her office. She was currently prepping a case that could possibly make or break her opportunity to make partner. More now than ever, she was stressed about her performance as an attorney. I called Shelley's office to update her on my recent plans. As I expected, she gave me her blessings and well wishes with the expansion. While I had her on the phone, I had to remind her that she was in her first trimester and to take it easy. She told me the trial was in less than twenty-four hours and that she would take a little time off once it was over.

The morning of the trial, Shelley had extreme morning sickness. Eli had been at the hospital for the past few days, so she had not had a chance to tell him about the pregnancy. She made it to the courtroom just in time for the case. The trial lasted the entire first half of the day. By 2:00 p.m., the judge ruled that Shelley's client was guilty of all charges. The estimated sentence would be five to ten years. After the judge made his decision, Shelley looked at her client and said,

"I am sorry." She also turned to her client's family, who was in attendance at the trial, and said sorry. All of their eyes were full of tears and disappointment. Shelley's client was then escorted out of the courtroom.

When Shelley arrived back at the office, Mr. Miller was waiting for her in the lobby area. He immediately told Shelley that they needed to talk, and they proceeded to walk into Mr. Miller's office. The conversation lasted about twenty-five minutes, and immediately following, Shelley left with a sense of relief.

For the first time in a while, Shelley was home before 5:00 p.m. She walked into the house, and Eli was sitting in the family room waiting for her. Without a word being said,

Shelley walked over to her husband and hugged him. Eli told her he made dinner plans for them and Mason would be with the nanny. With a smile, she hugged her husband once again. When Shelley walked into the bedroom, she noticed a black, thin-strapped cocktail dress lying on the bed. She turned to look at Eli and said, "Thank you."

Eli replied, "This is one of several surprises for you this evening."

Shelley grinned and said, "I have a surprise for you too."

Shelley and Eli had reservations at Chima Brazilian Steak House. As soon as they were seated, once again, Shelley told Eli that she had a surprise for him. She reached into her purse to pull out her sonogram, and placed it into Eli's hand. He looked at the sonogram, then at Shelley. "We're having a baby?"

Shelley replied, "Yes."

As expected, he was excited about the news. After both Shelley and Eli took in the pregnancy news, she had one more thing to discuss. She looked her husband in the eye and said, "I didn't make partner. They told me that while I was good at what I do, I wasn't partner material. After all I had put in and this is it. They said if I keep on working, maybe next year I can be considered again."

Eli replied by saying "good."

Shelley had a complete look of confusion on her face. She had expected him to at least sympathize with her; he knew how much her career meant to her.

Eli reached into his pocket and handed Shelley a box that was wrapped perfectly in gold metallic paper. Still with a confused look, Shelley started to take off the gold metallic wrapping paper, being careful not to completely destroy it. She opened the box, and there was a key inside. She looked at her husband and asked, "What's this?"

Eli replied, "Baby, you work so hard and never complain. I want you to be happy, and you're not at your firm. You spent years helping Mr. Miller build his company so now it is time to build your own. This key is to your new office so you can start your own law firm. I want you to follow the dream you always have, to be your own boss and be at the apex of your career."

Shelley looked at Eli with tears of joy. The day had begun with a sad note but it was now ending with happiness. When she had been told that she would not make partner, it had killed her for a moment, then she felt a sense of relief. Afterwards, she had wondered how she would move on. Here was the answer to the question that had boggling her mind.

She reached for his hand with a smile on her teary face. "Eli, I love you so much. Words cannot express how happy and appreciative I am. Thank you."

Eli kissed her on the lips. "You have been an awesome wife and mother Shelley. What more can I ask for? I will do anything for you. To make you happy and to wipe the frown that you have been having for a while now off your face. Now let's celebrate the beginning of a new dawn."

They finished eating their celebratory dinner and then headed home to enjoy the remainder of the evening.

# 11
# MEETING ADJOURNED

*There comes a day when you realize turning the*

*page is the best feeling in the world — because you*

*realize there's so much more to the book than the*

*page you were stuck on.*

*—Author Unknown*

Before leaving for Los Angeles, I had to meet up with Shelley for a quick lunch. Between our busy schedules, I hadn't had a chance to let her know about me flying out to LA. Shelley asked if we could meet at her house for lunch, and I agreed. In my head, I was thinking how unusual it was to have lunch at her house during the week, but I went over anyway. With a big smile on her face, Shelley was waiting for me on the porch to let me in. We walked in the house, and I immediately asked her why she was home this time of day and why she asked to have lunch at the house. Typically, during lunch, she would be stuck in her office working on a case of hers or Mr. Miller's. She poured us both a glass of chilled sweet tea, and then we made ourselves comfortable on the couch.

"So, Shelley, why exactly are you home this time of the day?" I asked.

Shelley snickered and said, "Because I resigned from the firm."

At this point, I was giving her a complete blank stare. It was unbelievable and I thought I had heard wrong.

Shelley snickered and said again, "I left the firm . . . to start my own."

I knew I had not heard wrong the first time. "What happened?" I asked in excitement. It seemed so much had happened since the last time I had called her which had just been two days ago talking about the case she had.

She updated me on her life's current events. She told me that Eli surprised her with the keys to her own office space so she could start her own practice. I guess at this point, a few of my doubts about Eli may have flown out the window, the joy on my friend's face was something I had not seen in a long time, she was truly happy. Immediately, I remembered the conversation we had about her branching out on her own. I was completely excited for Shelley and I told her of me and Marcel heading to LA for a few days.

We held on to each other close to tears at how far we had come even with the obstacles we had encountered. She was starting her firm as well as expecting a child and I was making my dream, my business bigger. We were damn happy about the women we were becoming, ones not confined to the standard of the society and ready to break barriers.

It was finally time for Marcel and me to board our flight to LA. We got settled in our seats, ordered a drink, and prepped for takeoff. The six-and-a-half-hour flight provided plenty of time for us to review the building contract and look at office furniture online. I found a thrift store located on the outskirts of LA which had furniture that would be perfect for the office. The store was in high demand, so I had to look online to be sure what I liked was still available. After the plane took off and we were clear to use electronic devices, Marcel and I took out our laptops and started working.

Two hours into the flight, I could feel Marcel staring at me. I looked over and asked him why he was looking at me like that. He leaned over to me and said, "You are beautiful. I've been wanting to say that to you for a long time."

Completely caught off guard, I replied with a simple thank you. The crazy thing was that, since I first met Marcel, I always thought he was attractive, well-groomed, and an overall well-kept man. He was also very successful in his law firm. Shelley had suggested I went out with him but I had not taken her seriously, until now.

My therapy sessions with Dr. Alexandria had been helping me be more open to men and accepting them with open arms. After the relationship with Josiah, I became guarded. Because of that, any other man that attempted to date me, failed. But now I had set myself free, my heart was willing to let someone in.

For the final three hours of the flight, Marcel and I talked about our past relationships, our families, how I branched out of corporate, and our futures in general. We always had a great business relationship, which also developed into a friendship, so talking to him had always been easy and natural to me. It felt good to have a conversation with someone who understood me and could complement me all at the same time. Our talk made the flight seem shorter than it really was. We finally landed in LAX, and our first stop was to go by the hotel to drop off our bags, and then we would go straight to the office space.

The office was beautiful; it was exactly what I envisioned. I joined Marcel and the building owners to finalize our paperwork and receive my keys. After about thirty minutes, all the documentation was signed. As I stared out the window with the most amazing view, it reminded me of serenity. This particular moment, I was thankful for overcoming the many challenges life has brought me, from my failed career in corporate America and a failed relationship that almost broke me, to having a successful advertising agency and a support system that I can count on. During my moment, Marcel walked over to me, placed his arms around my waist, and leaned in for a kiss. That was what I needed. He was what I needed.